Sophie's Knapsack

BY CATHERINE STOCK

LOTHROP, LEE & SHEPARD BOOKS • NEW YORK

Library of Congress Cataloging in Publication
Data Stock, Catherine. Sophie's knapsack.
Summary: Sophie accompanies her parents
on an overnight hike to Purple Cloud Rock.
[1. Hiking—Fiction]   I. Title.
PZ7.S8635Sp   1988 [E]   87-3103
ISBN 0-688-06457-4
ISBN 0-688-06458-2 (lib. bdg.)
Printed in Hong Kong.

For my hiking buddies —
Maggie and Robert

One day, Sophie and her father were looking out the window.

"It's time to show you some real sky, Sophie," said Daddy. "Let's hike up to Purple Cloud Rock next week."

Sophie's mother took her to buy a red knapsack and a blue sleeping bag.

The night before they left, Sophie packed warm socks, a sweater, and some snacky things to eat into her knapsack. She was very excited.

Sophie and her mother and father left the city early the next morning. They were far into the countryside when the sun came up.

"Here's a cup of hot cocoa and a cinnamon doughnut for you, Sophie," said Mother.

They arrived at the park at noon and set off down the trail.

"I feel like a tortoise carrying his house on his back," said Sophie.

The trail led through a meadow
filled with yellow and purple
blossoms. A blue dragonfly
fluttered over Sophie's head.

"'Sing Ho for the life of a Bear!'"
Daddy sang out.

They came to a clear blue lake.
"Let's pitch the tent under
those pine trees," said Mother.
It was getting chilly. Sophie
took her sweater out of her knapsack
and collected pinecones for a campfire.

They had beef noodle soup
and thick slices of bread and cheese
for supper. The warm fire crackled
lazily.

"Look, Sophie," said Mother,
"there's the Big Dipper."

"Mmmmm," mumbled Sophie
sleepily.

Sophie woke up the next morning to the smell of sizzling bacon. She scrambled out of her sleeping bag.

An eagle circled slowly above the lake. Suddenly, it dropped into the water and caught a fish.

"Aha, someone is having trout for breakfast," said Daddy.

After breakfast they carefully put out the fire and set off again.

"Lead the way, Sophie," said Mother.

A rabbit skidded across the path ahead of them and disappeared into the bushes.

Insects buzzed in the hot morning sun.

"This is *steep*," puffed Sophie.

"Not much farther," said Daddy. "Need a ride?"

"I'm okay, thanks," said Sophie.

Finally they arrived at the top
of Purple Cloud Rock. All around
them was nothing but blue sky
and wispy white clouds.

"It feels like the top of the world!"
said Sophie.

Daddy passed around a flask of lemonade. Sophie found a box of animal crackers at the bottom of her knapsack to share with her mother and father.

That night it rained. Sophie listened to the thud of raindrops on the side of their tent. She snuggled down into her warm, dry sleeping bag.

The ground was damp the next morning, but the sun was out again. The trail back to the car had lots of sploshy puddles.

Sophie took off her knapsack and settled down for the drive home. The knapsack was splattered with mud and full of cracker crumbs, but the fresh green scent of pinecones kept Sophie company all the way back to the city.